Bella of Madison Park

Leslie Stark

Archway Publishing books may be ordered through booksellers or by contacting:

Archway Publishing
1663 Liberty Drive
Bloomington, IN 47403
www.archwaypublishing.com
1 (888) 242-5904

Because of the dynamic nature of the Internet, any web addresses or links contained in this book may have changed since publication and may no longer be valid. The views expressed in this work are solely those of the author and do not necessarily reflect the views of the publisher, and the publisher hereby disclaims any responsibility for them.

ISBN: 978-1-4808-2984-8 (sc)
ISBN: 978-1-4808-2985-5 (e)

Print information available on the last page.

Archway Publishing rev. date: 5/10/2016

There once was a girl with a tail with a curl called Bella of Madison Park.

She was small and petite with four tiny white feet and at times she had a loud bark.

She sat in the window, watching the world
and everyone stopped to look

at the tiny blonde girl
with the tail with the curl
perched daintily on the nook.

In her pink winter coat
she braved all sorts of weather —
a hole for her tail that stuck out like a feather.

Everyone said, "she's the queen of the park,"
that girl with the curl and the very loud bark.

She guarded her people by day and by night,
she made sure to protect them with all of her might.

On hot summer days
she would prance and play,
and down by the lake she liked to stay.

She swam in the water,
she climbed on the rocks,
her fluffy tail wagged
as she played near the docks.

"Bella!" her master would call her by name,
and she always obeyed, and was glad she came.

Then one fine day Bella spotted a squirrel,
she quickly gave chase, and ran off in a whirl.

Far and away Bella ran down the block,
but the squirrel got away, he took off like a shot.

The sky turned to night and the ground had a frost,
it was then Bella knew that indeed she was lost.

Alone in the dark Bella heard a small sound,
she was startled and carefully looked around.

"Where are you going?" she heard a voice say.
And she looked up to see... a giant bluejay.
"Home!" Bella cried, "but I don't know the way."

"Come with me" said the jay, and he spread his wings wide.
Little Bella hopped on and they went for a ride.

Over trees and houses they flew in the dark,
til they reached Bella's house down in Madison Park.

"How can I thank you?" she said to the bird.
"Theres no need," he replied, "just remember my words:
Stay close to your master and don't stray from home,
and always remember you're never alone."

The jay smiled and said, "you're the queen of the park,
the girl with the curl and the very proud bark."

As her fluffy tail wagged with joy and delight,
the jay gave a wink, then flew out of sight.